Dreams Come True Forever

A GOLDEN BOOK • NEW YORK

ISBN: 978-0-7364-2399-1

www.randomhouse.com/kids/disney

Printed in the United States of America

30 29 28 27 26

Walt Disney's Cinderella

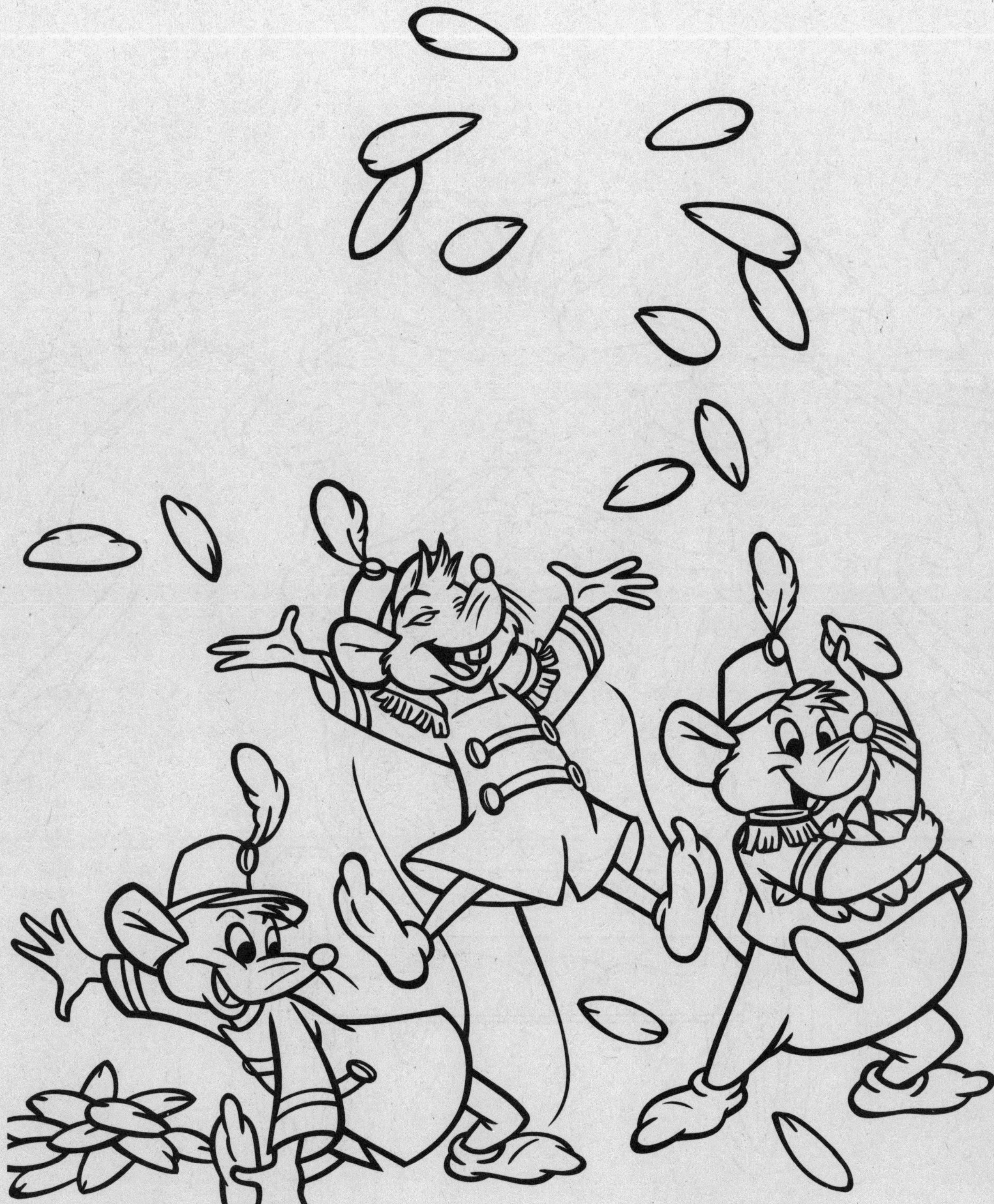

Walt Disney's
Sleeping Beauty

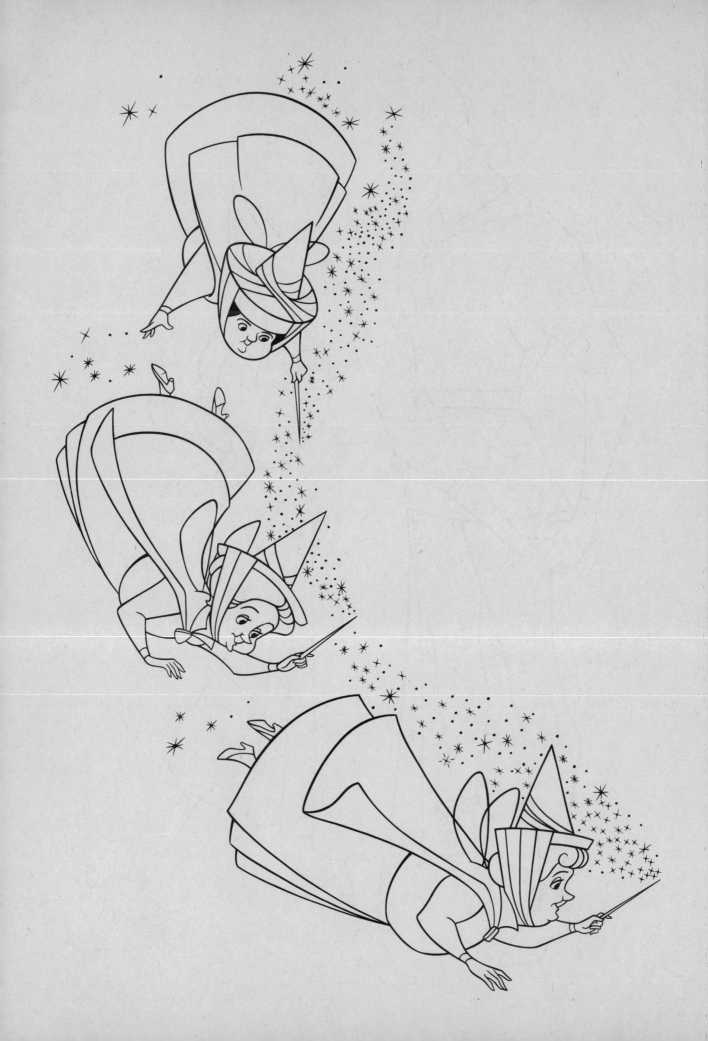

Walt Disney's

Snow White and the Seven Dwarfs

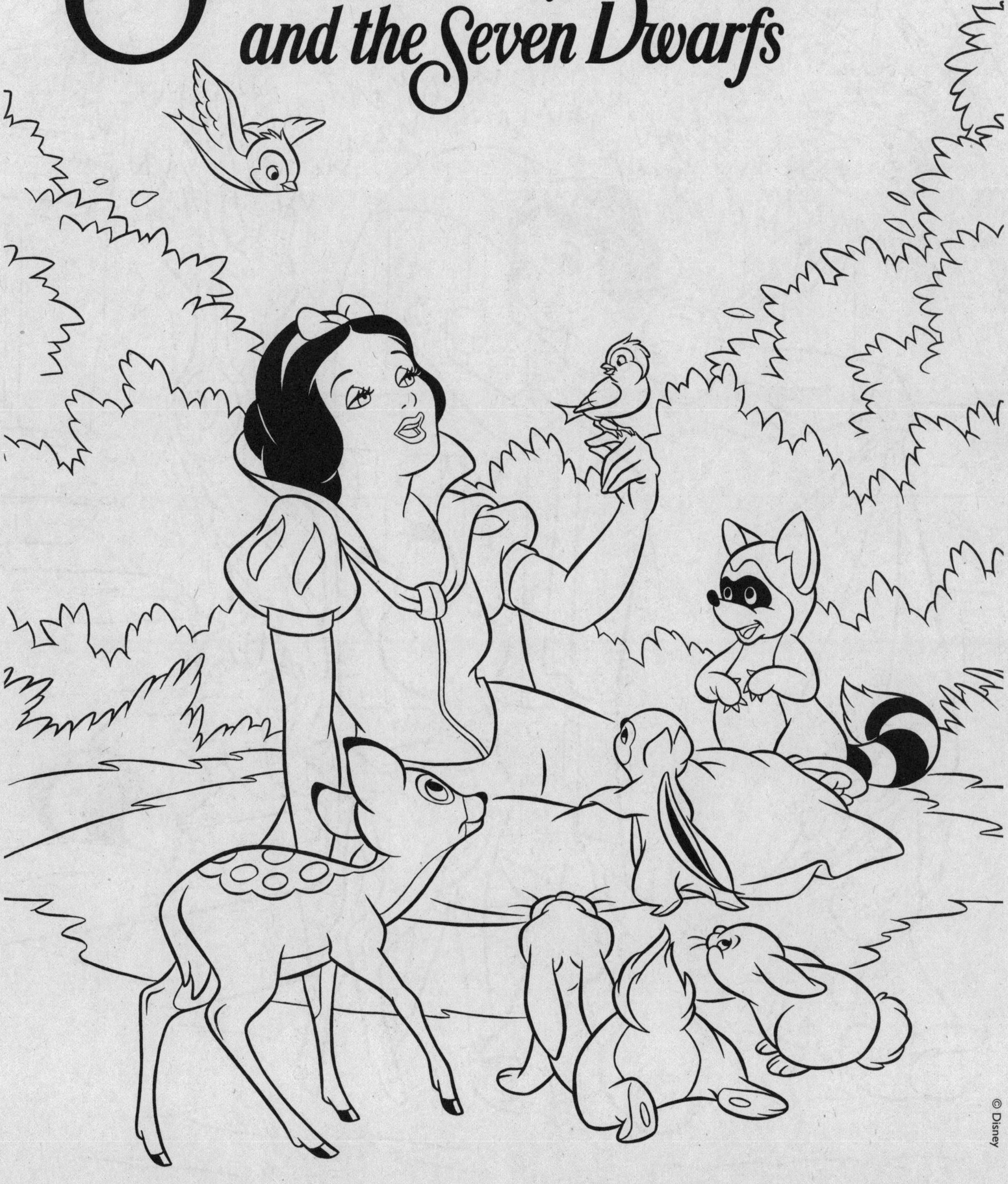

© Disney

PUZZLE MAGIC

It's Great to Be a Princess

What are the four things that every princess likes? To find out, write the letter beneath each flower on the circle on the first blank of each line. Then write every second letter in the circle in the rest of the blanks.

1 ___ ___ ___ ___ ___ ___

2 ___ ___ ___ ___ ___ ___ ___ ___

3 ___ ___ ___ ___ ___

4 ___ ___ ___ ___ ___ ___

Answers: 1. palace; 2. carriage; 3. tiara; 4. prince.

Where Is Snow White?

To find out, draw a line from each numbered
puzzle piece to the box where it belongs.

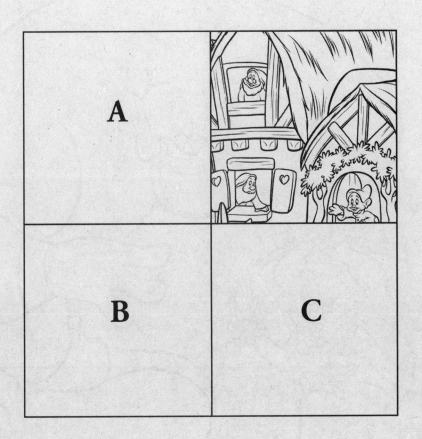

Presto Change-O!

Look at this page for one minute.
Then look at the next page and circle eight differences.

Answers: On this page, the Genie's hair is missing; the Genie has two wristbands; Jasmine has flowers around her waist; Jasmine has flowers around both wrists; the tall flowers are missing from Jasmine's hair; the stars are missing; the pattern is missing from the lamp; and Aladdin's vest is different.

Sweet Dreams

To find out what Ariel is dreaming about, write the letter beneath the arrow in the first blank. Then write every second letter in the rest of the blanks.

_ _ _ _ _ _ _ _ _ _ _ _ _ _

_ _ _ _ _ _ _ _

Pearls for a Princess

How many pearl necklaces can you count?

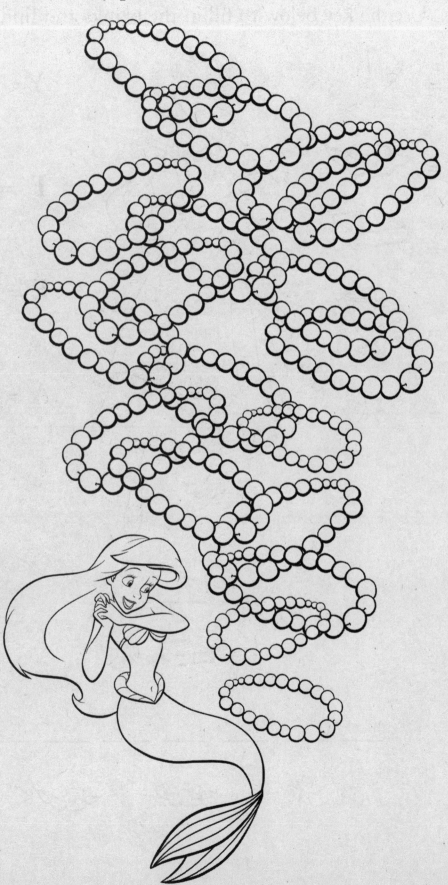

© Disney

Belle's Best

What is Belle's favorite room in the Beast's castle?
Use the key below to fill in the blanks and find out.

L =

R =

H =

B =

I =

Y =

T =

E =

A =

Celebration Under the Sea

Ariel has been invited to a special party. To find out what it is, cross out every letter that appears four or more times. Then write the remaining letters in the blanks from left to right.

P U T H E N

U M P E R U N M

A I P N D F E S

T P I N V U A L

_ _ _   _ _ _ _ _ _ _

_ _ _ _ _ _ _ _

Answer: The Mermaid Festival.

Bird Buzz

Finish each sentence by filling in the correct words from the list.
Then write each letter in the boxes that have the same numbers.

Word List
money • pictures • wags • food

1. A happy dog ___ ___ ___ ___ its tail.
                     1   2   3   4

2. When you're hungry, you eat ___ ___ ___ ___ .
                              5   6   7   8

3. You need ___ ___ ___ ___ ___ to buy things.
                 9   10   11   12   13

4. You use crayons to draw ___ ___ ___ ___ ___ ___ ___ ___ .
                         15   16   17   18   19   20   21   22

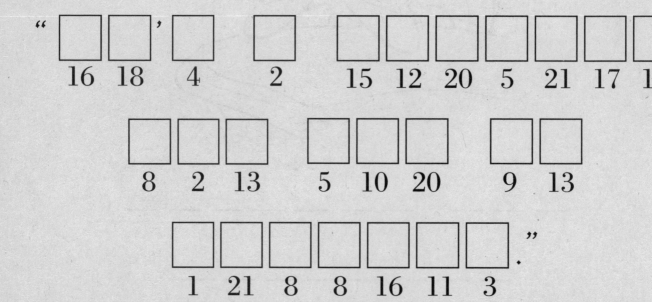

"☐ ☐ ' ☐   ☐   ☐ ☐ ☐ ☐ ☐ ☐ ☐
 16 18   4   2   15 12 20 5 21 17 18

☐ ☐ ☐   ☐ ☐ ☐   ☐ ☐
 8 2 13   5 10 20   9 13

☐ ☐ ☐ ☐ ☐ ☐ ☐ "
1 21 8 8 16 11 3 .

Search for Seven

Circle the names of all the Seven Dwarfs in the puzzle below.
Look up, down, forward, backward, and diagonally.

♡ Sleepy ♡ Dopey ♡ Sneezy ♡ Happy

♡ Doc ♡ Grumpy ♡ Bashful

```
L T S M I H B R Y
S U I A N A H R E
X L F R G P T O P
Y P E H A P U G O
L Z C E S Y O R D
N O E R P A S U T
C U T E R Y B M L
Y E N I N L X P I
C O D X M S K Y N
```

© Disney

Answer:

Belle Loves Books

How many times is the word BOOK written in the puzzle below?
Look up, down, backward, and forward.

O K B O O K O O B O O K
K B O O K O O B K O O B
B O O K O O B O O K B O
O K O O B K O O B O O O
O K O O B O O K O O B K

Swim and Find

Look at this picture for one minute. Then turn the page to see if you can spot eight differences.

Lost in the Forest

Can you help the Prince find Snow White?

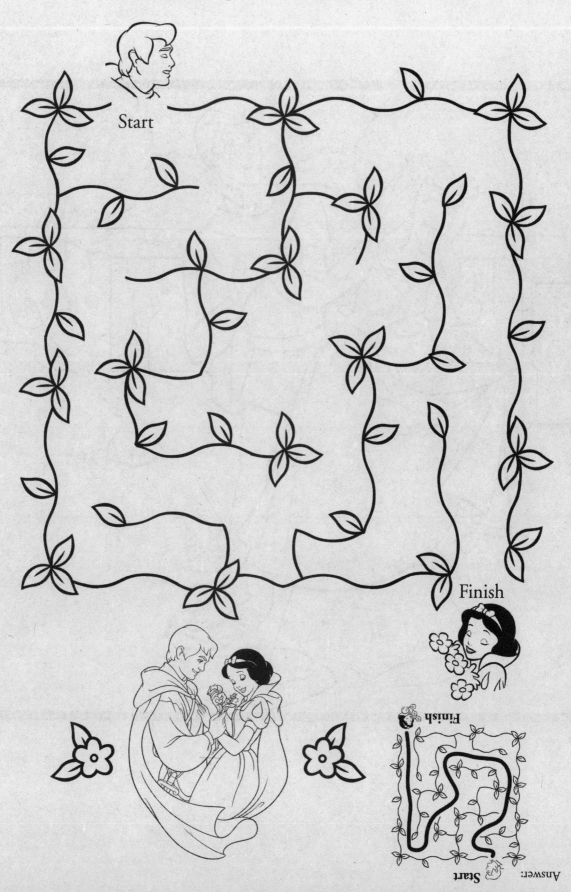

Start

Finish

Answer: Start Finish

Skipping Stones

Circle six things that are different in these pictures.

Answers: On this page, Aurora is not wearing a necklace; Phillip's belt buckle is missing; there is a bird on the last stone; there is one more stone; Phillip is wearing two medals; and Aurora does not have a flower in her hair.

Sky Riders

Where are Aladdin and Jasmine going? To find out, follow the line from each letter to a box and then write the letters in the boxes.

HTMOETKRATE

□□ □ □□ □□ □□ □□□□□ □□□□ □ !

Word Magic

How many words can you make out of MAGIC CARPET?
Write them below.

_____   _____

_____   _____

_____   _____

_____   _____

_____   _____

_____   _____

Possible answers: age, am, ape, are, ate, cage, cape, car, cat, get, grip, ice, it, map, mat, meat, page, part, pat, race, rat, ripe, tap, tape, tar, tea, tear, team.

Find Flounder!

Which line will take Ariel to Flounder?

Mrs. Potts's Party

Mrs. Potts is having a tea party for Belle and the Beast.
Look up, down, backward, forward, and diagonally
to find everything she needs for it.

♡ BOWL   ♡ DISH   ♡ GLASS   ♡ PLATE   ♡ SPOON
♡ CUP   ♡ FORK   ♡ NAPKIN   ♡ SAUCER   ♡ TEAPOT

```
E T A L K F O N R P
D K E S O N O P L L
I N L A P O I W O A
S I A L P B O F B T
H K T S W O D I E F
I P O P L A T E D E
S A U C E R F L I D
H N O R P C W O F E
G L A S S O U L R A
P K N I B S G P S K
```

Answer:

Bubble Boxes

Take turns with a friend drawing lines between two bubbles.
If you make a box, put your initials in it and give yourself a
point. Boxes with Sebastian or Flounder are worth three points.
Boxes with Ariel are worth four points. When you can't make
any more boxes, the person with more points wins.

Magical Makeover

Look at this picture for one minute. Then turn the page to see if you can spot eight differences.

Fairy Helpers

Use the code to find out the names of Aurora's three fairy helpers.

A	B	C	D	E	F	G	H	I	J	K	L	M	N	O	P	Q	R	S	T	U	V	W	X	Y	Z
26	25	24	23	22	21	20	19	18	17	16	15	14	13	12	11	10	9	8	7	6	5	4	3	2	1

1. ___ ___ ___ ___ ___
    21 15 12 9 26

2. ___ ___ ___ ___ ___
    21 26 6 13 26

3. ___ ___ ___ ___ ___ ___ ___ ___ ___ ___ ___ ___
    14 22 9 9 2 4 22 26 7 19 22 9

Answers: 1. Flora; 2. Fauna; 3. Merryweather.

Giving Friends

The forest birds have a gift for Snow White.
Can you find the two that match?

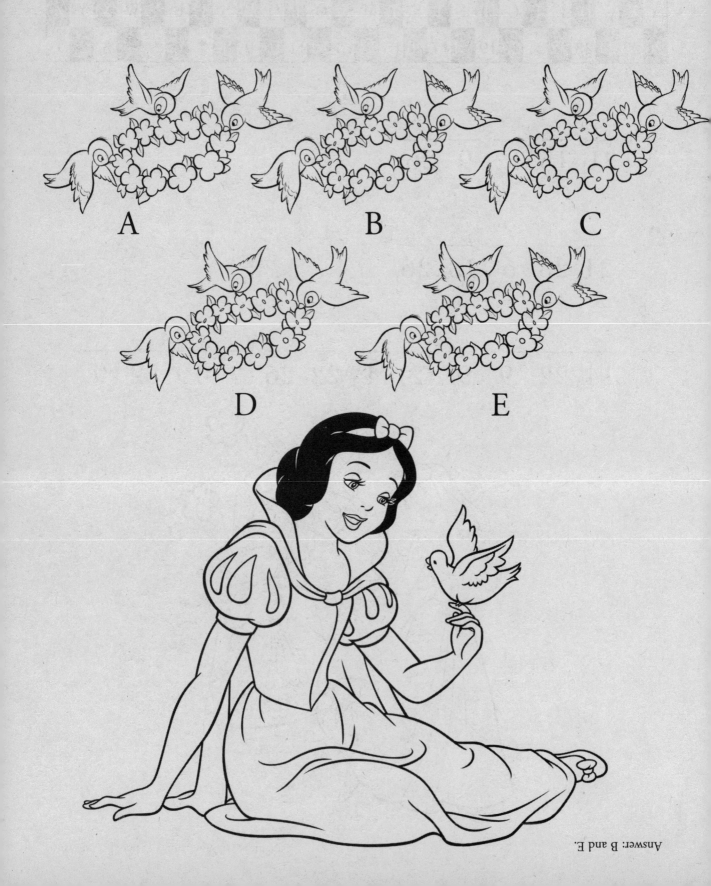

A

B

C

D

E

Ready for the Ball

Circle everything Cinderella needs for the ball.
Look up, down, backward, forward, and diagonally.

♡ FLOWERS   ♡ INVITATION   ♡ SHOES   ♡ PERFUME
♡ HORSES   ♡ GLOVES   ♡ NECKLACE   ♡ GOWN

```
N A M K C A S E R N
R E F T Z I E P S O
A T C R I K O L E I
I N G K N E H A S T
L O L X L M S E R A
U G O W N A R N O T
R E V I B Y C F H I
E K E M U F R E P V
L M S O S T E R A N
S R E W O L F N E I
```

Answer:

Under the Sea Is the Place to Be

Fill in the blanks with the words that rhyme with SEA.

1. It unlocks a door. ___ ___ ___

2. It makes honey. ___ ___ ___

3. You drink it hot or iced. ___ ___ ___

4. You put one on each foot to slide through the snow. ___ ___ ___

5. It has branches and leaves. ___ ___ ___ ___

A-Mazing Journey

Help Aladdin find his way to Jasmine.

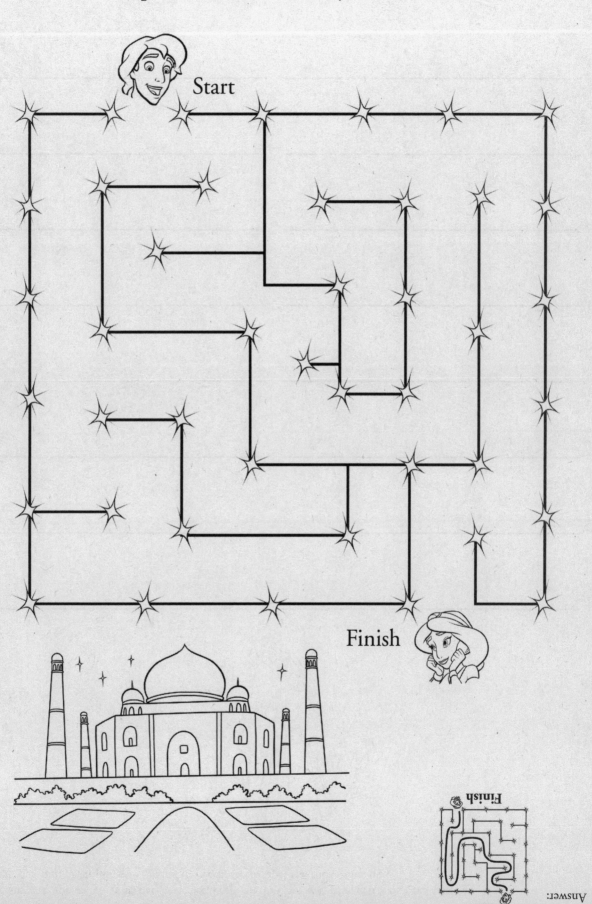

Start

Finish

Answer:

Start

Finish

Name Game

How many words can you make from SLEEPING BEAUTY?

_____   _____

_____   _____

_____   _____

_____   _____

_____   _____

_____   _____

_____   _____

_____   _____

Tea for Three

Look at this picture for one minute.
Then turn the page to see if you can spot eight differences.

A Special Spot

Cinderella is making a gift for some friends.
Follow each spool of thread to the end.
To find out what the gift is, write the letters
from the spools in the spaces.

D   B   E   A

___ ___ ___ ___

Bed Buddies

To find out who the bed is for, use the code below.

26	25	24	23	22	21	20	19	18	17	16	15	14	13	12	11	10	9	8	7	6	5	4	3	2	1
A	B	C	D	E	F	G	H	I	J	K	L	M	N	O	P	Q	R	S	T	U	V	W	X	Y	Z

___ ___ ___   ___ ___ ___   ___ ___ ___
20   6   8   26   13   23   17   26   10

Time for Bed!

Find all the bedtime words in the puzzle below.
Look up, across, and backward.

Word List

PILLOW   BED
BLANKET   NIGHT
DREAM   SLEEP

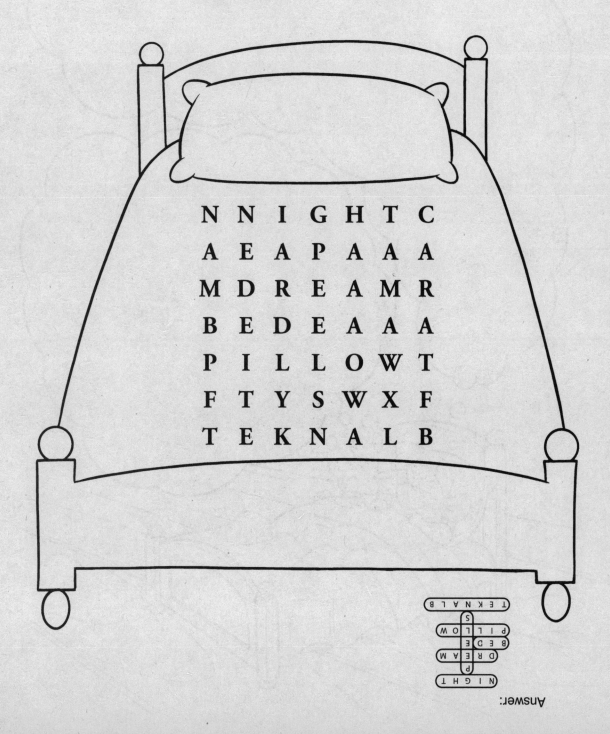

```
N  N  I  G  H  T  C
A  E  A  P  A  A  A
M  D  R  E  A  M  R
B  E  D  E  A  A  A
P  I  L  L  O  W  T
F  T  Y  S  W  X  F
T  E  K  N  A  L  B
```

Answer:

Sweet Dreams

Gus and Jaq are dreaming about their friend Cinderella.
Draw their dreams in the bubbles below.

Skipping Stones

Gus and Jaq have something for Cinderella, too.
Color the stones that spell GIFT so they can reach her.

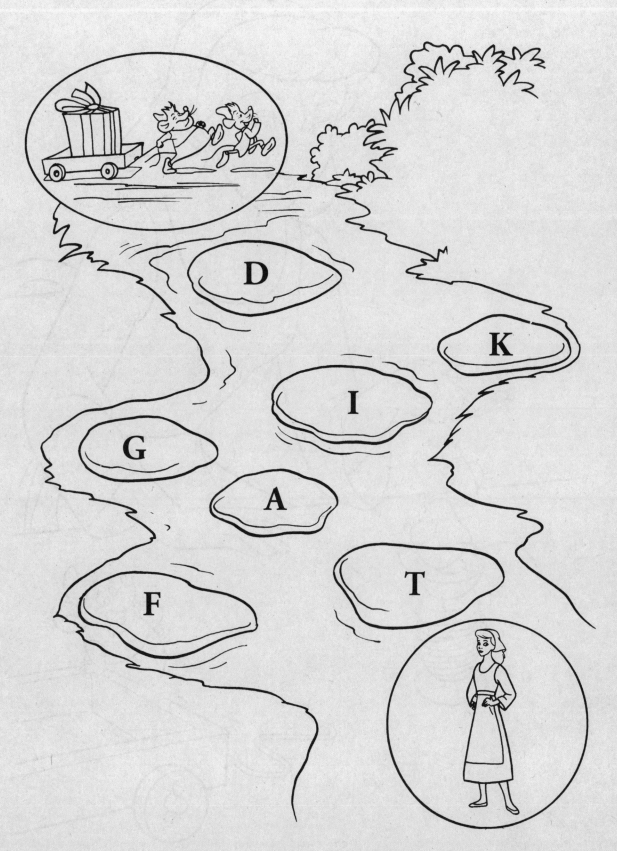

Cinderella loves her new thimble.
Gus and Jaq hope she'll use it to make them more gifts!

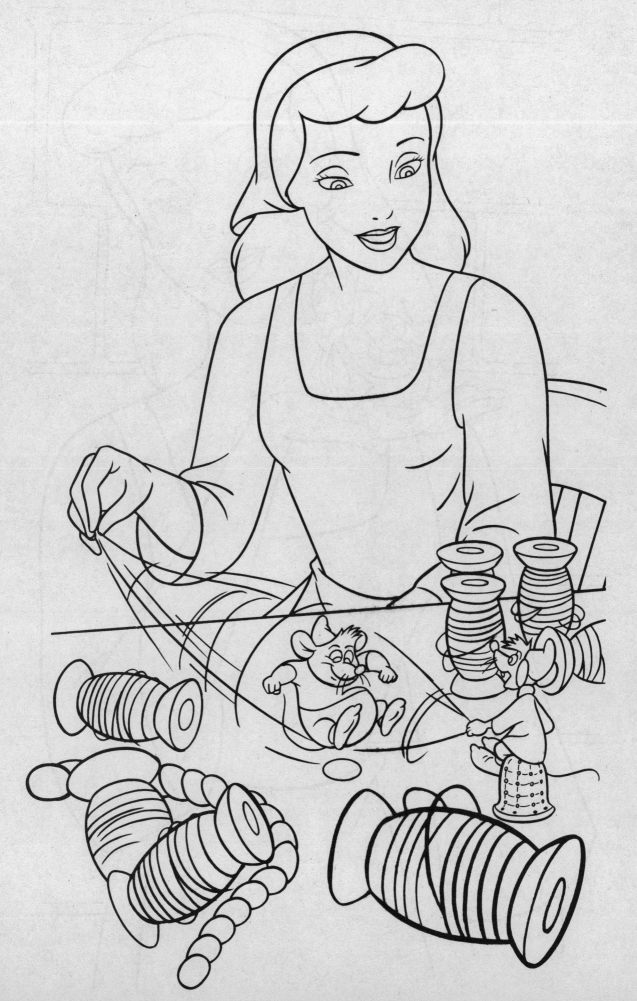

"What should I do today?" Ariel wonders.

"I'm going to look for Flounder to play a game with me!"
Find all the letters in **FLOUNDER** hidden in the plants.

Name Game

Ariel plays a game while she looks for Flounder.
How many words can you help her make
from the letters in **FLOUNDER**?

_____   _____

_____   _____

_____   _____

_____   _____

_____   _____

_____   _____

Possible answers: den, do, end, fun, loud, no, or, red, rod, round, run, under.

"I was looking for you, but you found me!"

Follow the Leader

Help Ariel and Flounder follow the music to Sebastian.

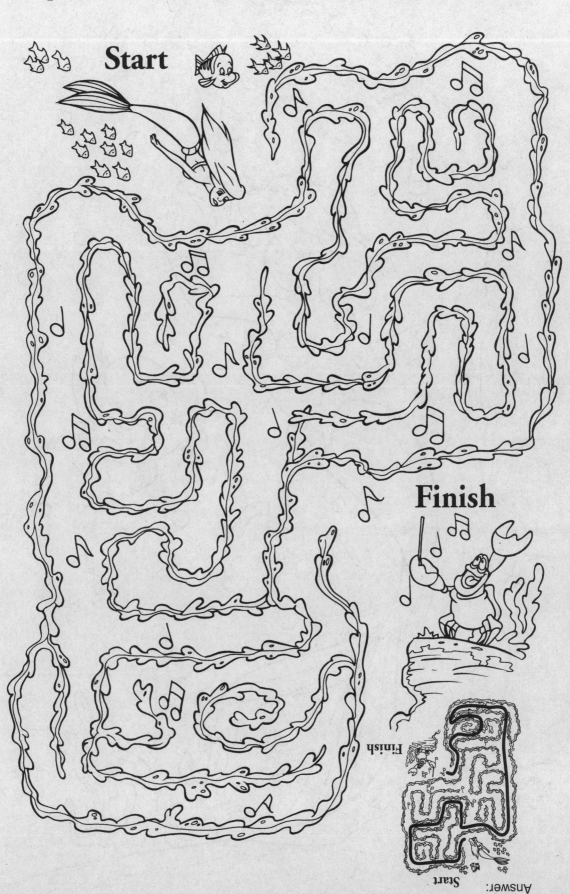

They made it!

Belle is planning a surprise birthday party for a good friend.

Mrs. Potts makes sure the food is just right.

Lumiere makes sure the castle is decorated.
Use the key to color the balloons.

KEY
1 = green   2 = yellow   3 = blue
4 = red   5 = purple

Who could the party be for?
Match each gift in the picture to the one below.
Write the letter from the matching gift on the space to find out.

____   ____   ____   ____

"Chip's our guest!"

"Enjoy your feast!"

"Open your gifts!"

"This is the best surprise ever!"

Jasmine is going to the marketplace to look for flowers.

Rajah will go with her.

"There are some beautiful flowers here!"

Flower Power

How many flowers can you count?

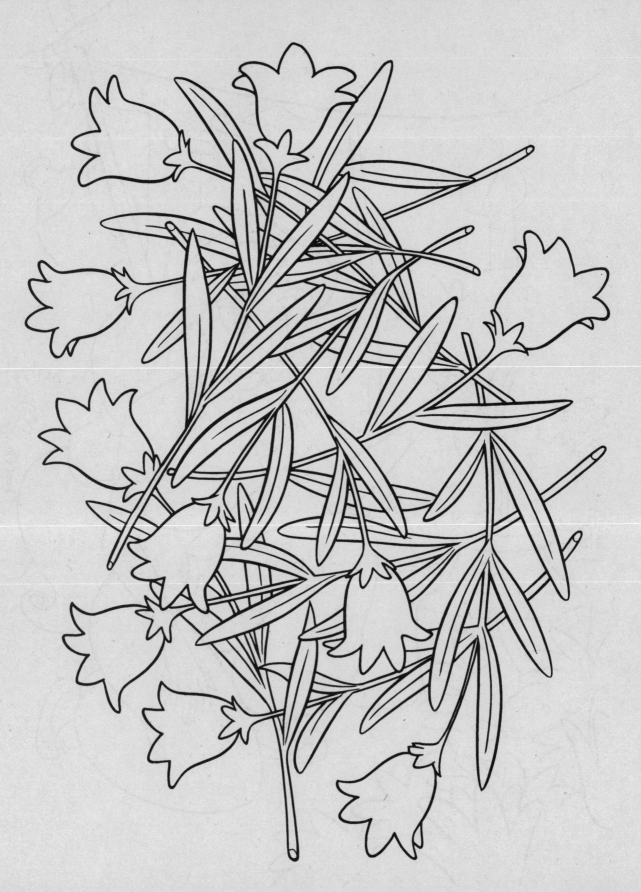

Jasmine thinks Rajah looks like a king in his flower crown.

Rajah has something special for his friend Jasmine . . .

. . . and Jasmine has a special hug for him!

Rajah is a loyal friend who looks very royal.

Singing birds, blooming flowers . . .
spring is in the air!

"I think we should do some spring cleaning and tidy up the castle!"
says Belle to Beast.

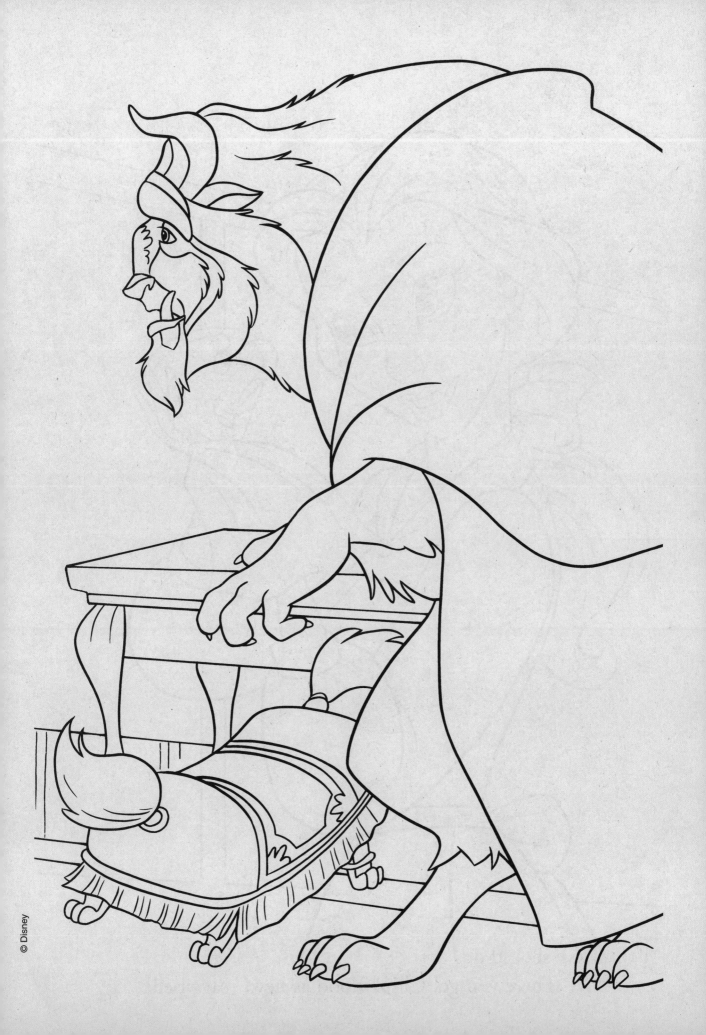

"There you go, Chip! Good as new!" says Belle.

"Ooh! Ooh! That tickles!"
"Hold still, Cogsworth. This hour hand is almost fixed."

"I read these books so much, they hardly ever get dusty. Still, I want them to look perfect!" says Belle.

"Belle will be surprised by all the colorful flowers
I have planted for her," says Beast.

"You look beautiful, Footstool!"

Crystal clear!

"I didn't know we had so many things!"
growls Beast.

The enchanted silverware and dishes take a bath. Soon they'll be sparkling clean!

Belle picks out her favorite dress and fixes her hair.

Beast gets dressed up, too!

A shiny Lumiere lights a special spring dinner.

Dinner is served!

A perfect spring evening!

Love at First Sight

Ariel lives underwater in Atlantica.

How many fish can you find?

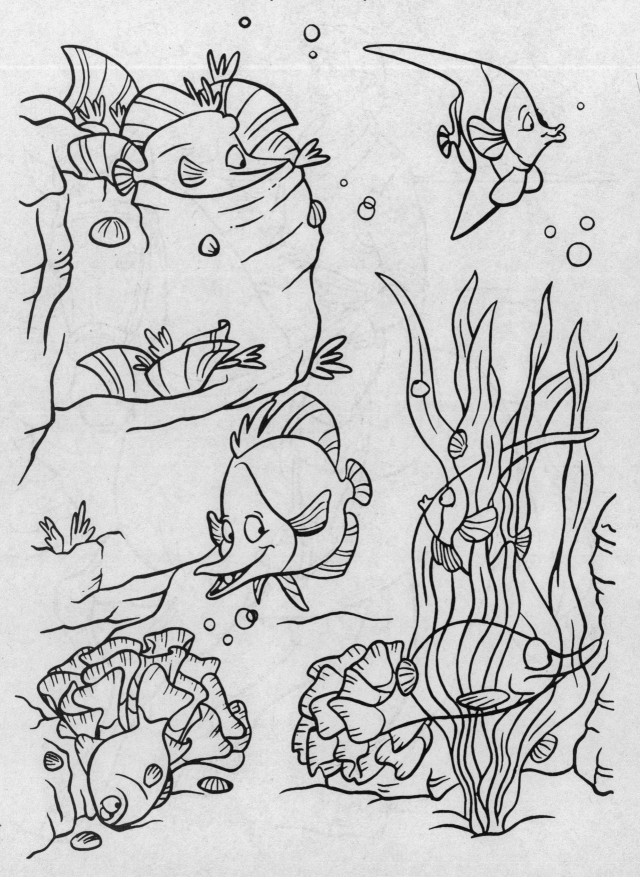

Answer: 6.

Eric lives on land.

Who lives on land? Who lives in the sea?
Label each animal: **L = land, S = sea.**

Ariel loves things from the human world.

She collects treasures from the land.
How many does she have?

Answer: 16.

Ariel's favorite treasure is a statue . . .

. . . of Eric!

When Ariel sees Eric's ship . . .

. . . it's love at first sight!

Eric's music gets Ariel's attention.

When Eric is tossed overboard, Ariel saves his life!

Ariel daydreams about Eric.

Hold this page up to a mirror to see what Ariel is thinking.

I LOVE YOU, ERIC!

Have a grown-up help you cut out the puzzle pieces.
Put the pieces together to make a picture.
Then tape the backs of the pieces in place and color
Ariel and Eric!

Ariel is thinking about Eric.
Use the blank grid to help you draw your own picture of Eric.

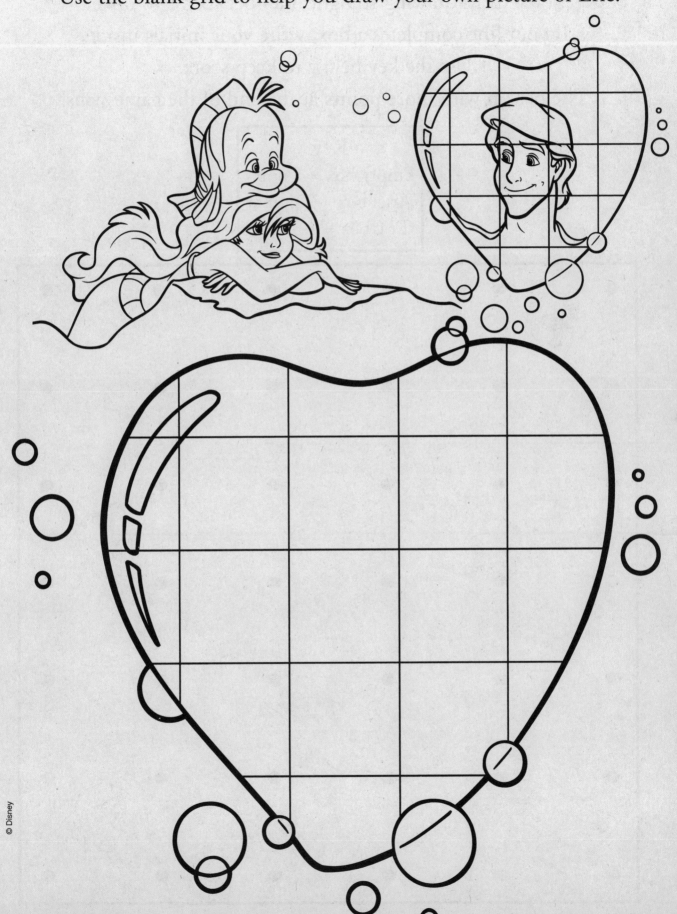

A Lovely Game for You and a Friend!

Take turns drawing straight lines between two dots.
If your line completes a box, write your initials inside.
Use the key below to keep score.
The person with more points at the end of the game wins!

Key
Empty box = 1 point
Ariel box = 2 points
Eric box = 3 points

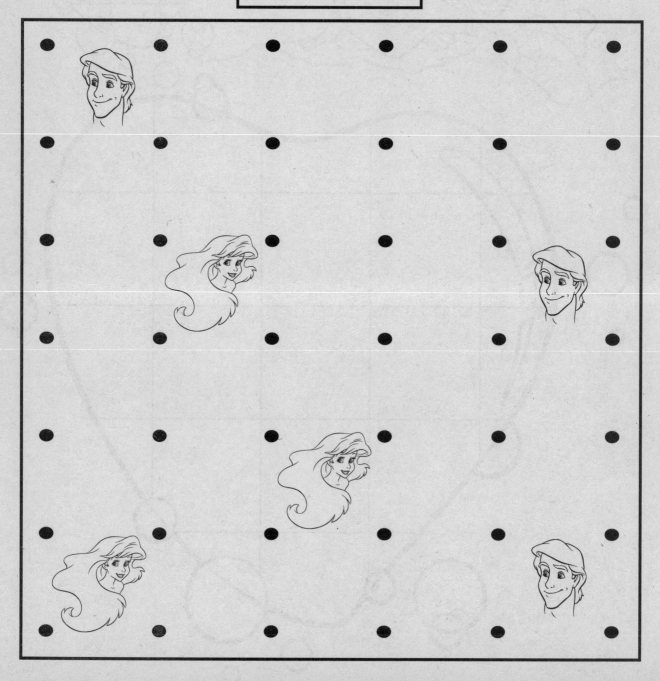

Play again!

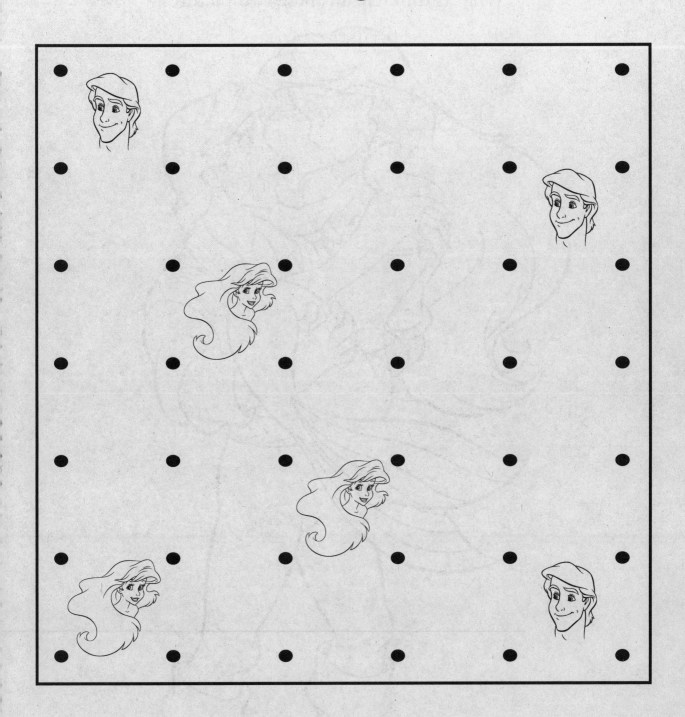

Spot the Differences
What is different in these two pictures?

How much does Ariel love Eric?
Count the hearts!

When Ariel's tail turns into legs,
she can walk on the beach with Eric!

Sebastian loves making mood music.

A romantic ride to remember!

Help Ariel follow the trail to Eric.

Finish

Start

Ariel and Eric are getting married!
Help decorate their wedding invitation.
When you are done, have a grown-up help you cut it out and fold
it in half.

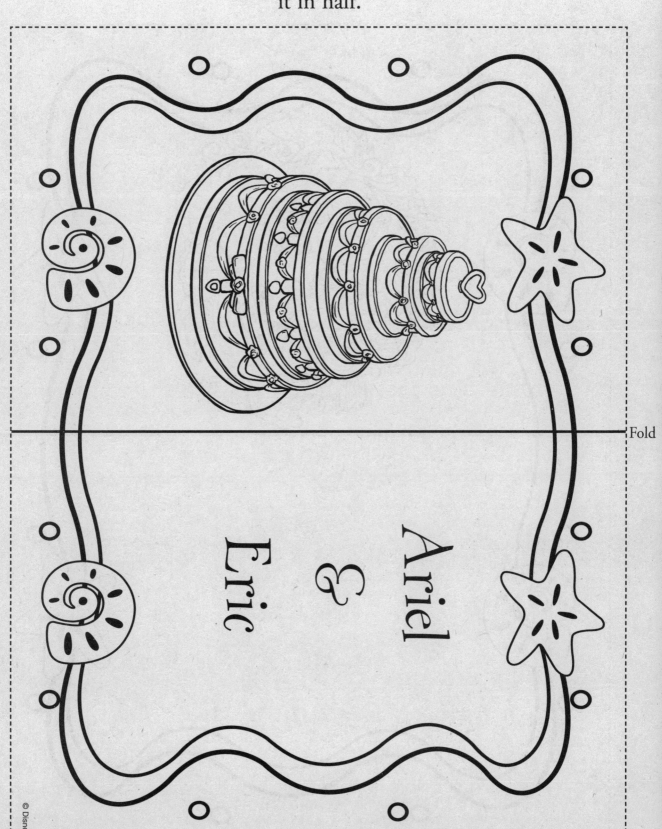

Fold

Fold

A Perfect Party!

Find everything that starts with P at Ariel
and Eric's wedding party.

Answers: parrot, pears, plates, plant.

A royal wedding!

Dream Dance

Cinderella lives with her mean stepfamily.

Decorate Cinderella's pillow, curtain, and nightgown.

Cinderella helps with all kinds of chores.

But she has friends who pitch in.

Cinderella wonders what it would be like to meet a prince.

Add more flowers to Cinderella's basket.

One day, an invitation to the Royal Ball arrives.

Cinderella's stepsisters argue over who should read it first.

You Are Invited
to a Royal Ball
at the Castle

Cinderella wants to go to the ball.

But she must stay home until all her chores are finished.

"We'll help you with your chores, Cinderelly," says Gus.

Jaq wants to help Cinderella with her chores.
Help him get to the bucket and brush.

Start

Finish

Finish

Start

Answer:

After finishing all her chores, Cinderella has no time
to get ready for the ball.

But her animal friends have a surprise.

They will make a dress for Cinderella to wear to the ball!

Help Cinderella's friends make a dress by adding a design.

Design your very own dress for Cinderella!

Cinderella's dress is ready!

Cinderella is ready for the ball!
Can you tell which two pictures are exactly alike?

A

B

C

D

Answer: B and D.

The Perfect Prince

Find the words in the puzzle that describe the perfect prince for Cinderella. Look up, down, and from left to right.

Word List

Kind
Strong

Gentle
Brave

Smart
Honest

```
A H G C R M Q K
T O E W O H W I
G N N F S V A N
S E T J O E G D
M S L Z C N H L
A T E B R A V E
R D Y B F T D H
T I S T R O N G
```

Cinderella's wicked stepsisters have ruined her dress!

Now she'll never get to the ball to meet the Prince.

Suddenly, Cinderella's Fairy Godmother appears!

The Fairy Godmother is going to change
a pumpkin into a coach for Cinderella.
Help her find the pumpkin.

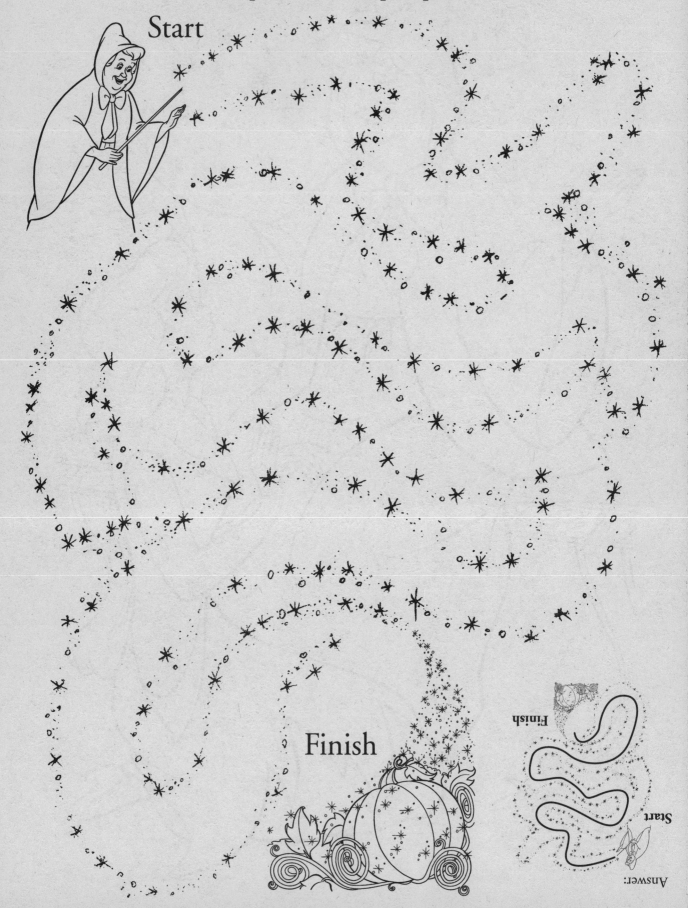

Start

Finish

Finish

Start

Answer:

With the wave of a wand, Cinderella has a beautiful gown.

Cinderella meets the Prince.
Her dream has come true!

A dream dance, and a night to remember!